Sweet Heart

Linda Lingle

May your life
always be poised on
the brink of
promise & possibility.

Lingle
4/12/19

ALL RIGHTS RESERVED

Publisher's Note:

This is a work of fiction. All names, characters, places, and events are the work of the author's imagination.

Any resemblance to real persons, places, or events is coincidental.

Solstice Publishing -
www.solsticepublishing.com

Sweet Heart

By

Linda Lingle

For R --

September 25, 2016

You often asked how I felt when we first met, and never tired of hearing the story, so I guess I should start with that. Did I feel the same rush of adrenalin, the same spark of electricity? And what was it about you that attracted me?

I remember the moment clearly. You were wearing a short-sleeved, black dress that fell just to your knees with black hose and black high heels to match. The combination was incredibly sexy. Had I known, then, that your nylons were not attached to a practical pair of panties, but were held close to your thighs with embroidered lace, it would have brought me to my knees.

A string of small pearls and matching earrings softened the look, like a contradiction. Your auburn hair was tied up in a loose bun at the crown of your head. Wisps of it fell to the side, framing your face. I wondered how long it would be if I released it and I wanted to do that, right then and there.

So, did I want you, in that instant, in the same way you've said that you wanted me? Oh, yeah. I could feel the heat surge into that part of my body that would belong to you.

This is going to be trouble, my boy, and you'd better steer clear, I thought to myself.

But it was already too late; I was a goner. All I wanted to do was run my hands along your thighs and explore all there was to discover under that black dress. But I knew that I wouldn't. For one thing, we would be working together, and for another, I was married, and so were you, according to the ring on your finger. And, although my marriage was in shambles, I figured yours must be intact. How could it not be? Surely, the lucky guy who possessed you must have been keeping you happy. But your smile was so warm and engaging that I imagined it was an invitation and I found myself hoping that it was.

I knew it was crazy, and probably nothing more than wishful thinking, on the part of a man who had long been denied the pleasures he expects to receive, on a more-or-less regular basis, when he marries. But I saw something in your eyes that promised the kind of completion and fulfillment that men fantasize about from the time they achieve reason, and I was drawn to that, like a bee to nectar; like a moth to a flame.

Even after all of these years, it still amazes me that we came together so quickly and I credit you for that. It was your hand that lingered in mine when we first shook at our introduction; your fingers that brushed against my palm like a feather as you handed me orientation materials; your knee that grazed mine as you situated in the chair next to me at that first morning conference, and then hovered so close that I could hardly breathe for anticipating another contact. You seemed fearless to me, like Amelia Earhart and Scarlett O' Hara and, although I didn't know what to make of you, I was intrigued and wanted more than anything to make some moves of my own, even though I was out of practice and, I was sure, out of my league.

I sought you out for perspective on my new accounts and leaned in so close, to peer at your computer screen that our cheeks nearly touched as you showed me how to access their files. I breathed in the aroma of your hair, pine woods and wildflowers from the Clairol Herbal Essence you used, and the scent of citrus and vanilla from the Emeraude cologne you dabbed behind your ears.

By the third day, I had worked up enough courage to let my leg sidle against yours under that long, walnut table, and stay put for the length of the morning conference. That you did not protest, or shift away, was unbelievable to me and I wondered if I should press my luck, even though I knew that I didn't have the steel for it.

The first weekend away from you was excruciating. I missed the lilt of your voice, the music of your laugh, and the smell of you that delighted, and overwhelmed, my senses. I passed the hours replaying our first days together in a continuous loop, examining every second of our time together and trying to make sense of it. Nothing like you had ever happened to me before and I was afraid; afraid that the long years of living in an emotional and sexual desert had clouded my judgment; afraid that I would overreach and end up disgraced and jobless, and afraid that, even if you welcomed my advances, at the moment of truth I would not measure up to your expectations. But the mere thought of intimacy with you sent shockwaves through my body that were so startling and strong, they eclipsed my fears and set me on a course that would change my life forever.

When I sat down next to you, for Monday's meeting, I could feel that the energy between us was charged with sexual tension. I knew that I would not make it through the day if I was not able to hold you and caress you and experience the feel of your lips on mine. But, even though I desperately wanted to be the Rhett to your Scarlett, I feared I was more like Walter Mitty, living a fantasy, and I just could not bring myself to take the next step. Defeated, and disappointed in myself, I left the office as soon as the meeting adjourned to take a walk and clear my head. That was when I discovered Florentina's.

September 28, 2016

Flo was sweeping the sidewalk in front of her restaurant and, with my head down and my attention focused back at the office and on you, I walked into her.

"What-sa matter you?" she demanded, upending her broom and holding it in front of her like a shield.

"Lovesick," I mumbled, sheepishly, hoping to avoid a scene.

"Ayeeee," she brayed. "Is miserable, no?"

I nodded. "Is miserable, yes."

"Come in," she invited, taking me by the hand and pulling me through the door. "Florentina have just the thing for you."

She led me to a table in the middle of the deserted restaurant then disappeared into her kitchen. In the next instant, she returned with a large bowl of Italian Wedding Soup and a small loaf of bread on a thick carving board hollowed out by the handle to hold a saucer of olive oil.

"So," Florentina asked, sitting down beside me. "Dis girl, she no love you?"

"I don't know," I admitted. "I just met her."

Florentina grinned. "Ah, is like thunderbolt, yes?"

I smiled at the thought. "Oh, yeah. It was a thunderbolt all right."

"Well, you bring her here and find out."

I looked around the room. It was warm and charming but far too public for what I had in mind. I shook my head.

"It's not as easy as that, Flo," I said. "There's a complication."

"You no worry about complication," she said. "I have just the thing."

And with that she got up and walked over to the curtained wall, drew back the fabric and revealed the booths in the alcove.

I dropped the spoon into my soup and stood up to get a better look. Slowly, I began to smile as I imagined the possibilities.

"Well," Florentina demanded, impatiently. "Is good, yes?"

I nodded. "Is very good."

Though obsessed with the thought of the shrouded booths and my fantasies of what we could experience there, it took me three days to get up the courage to ask you to lunch. That's how suave I was. And I doubt that I would have acted even then if the weekend, and the prospect of enduring two more days without experiencing the feel of you in my arms, hadn't loomed large and forlorn in front of me.

To tell you the truth, I didn't expect you to accept my invitation. I was convinced that I had totally misjudged a mild flirtation for something more carnal and was fully prepared to slink back to my office with my tail between my legs if you shot me down. When you didn't and, in fact, responded with enthusiasm, it was as if I had been fortified with a shot of single malt scotch, and a hearty chaser.

Having cleared the first hurdle, I immediately panicked. Now that I had the tiger by the tail, I had no damned idea what to do with it. But the thought of spending time alone with you in a place that offered enough seclusion to allow for the possibilities I dreamed about, spurred me on.

Putting my hand on the small of your back, to guide you across the street and down the alley out of sight of our office, was my test balloon. I wasn't sure what I would do if you rebuffed my advance, but I figured that the gesture was innocent enough that it wouldn't kill me, or my career, if you did. Still, I was braced for the worst, and emboldened when it didn't come. I allowed the tips of my fingers to skim yours as we walked and, when I heard the breath catch in your throat, I loosely entwined my fingers with yours and waited for all hell to break loose. To this day, I still consider it the best luck I ever had when your hand enfolded mine, firm and sure, letting me know that I could soon feel the crush of your lips on mine and end the agony of my pent up desire.

Wanting everything to be perfect, I had visited the restaurant the previous day and made arrangements with Florentina to reserve the curtained, corner booth, furthest from view. This delighted Flo to no end, so it was no surprise that she was waiting for us when we arrived. She looked you over with a critical eye, taking particular note of your hand holding tightly to mine. Nodding approvingly, she issued her verdict.

"Is good," she decreed.

I laughed. "Oh, yeah, Flo. Is very good!"

After we were seated, Florentina signaled to a waiter who was hovering nearby, and he hurried over and presented you with a spray of hydrangeas and daylilies and Shasta daisies, wrapped in damp paper towels and tin foil. Florentina had selected them herself, she told us proudly, from her own personal garden. You buried your face in the fragrant bouquet, then smiled up at Flo and thanked her, warmly.

As much as I appreciated Florentina's cordiality, more than anything, I wanted her to fade into the background so that I could be alone with you. I had been waiting for this moment for what seemed like an eternity, and I was eager for it to unfold. Sensing my impatience, Florentina laid our menus on the table, declared she had to check her sauce, and bustled quickly away, letting the wine and cheese themed curtain fall closed behind her.

When we came together, at last, it was everything I imagined it would be. I leaned across the table and looked inquiringly into your eyes. When you answered my unspoken question by leaning in to me, I cupped your face in my hands and, with a level of sophistication I didn't normally possess, I kissed you. I thought that even the ecstasy of intercourse could not surpass the thrill I felt when our lips finally met, not soft and sweet as one would think of a first kiss, but hard and strong, probing and primordial, as if we were already lovers, hungry for each other after a long separation.

Passion drove me from my side of the table to yours. With an uncharacteristic confidence, I pulled you to me with a commanding force that was immensely satisfying. Instinctively, my hand slid under your skirt and up your silky thigh. Then you caressed me through the fabric of my trousers and a low-throated groan escaped my lips, revealing the depth of my desire. If Florentina had not chosen that moment to come back with the soup, there's no telling what would have come next. How I ever mustered enough self-control to smile at Florentina and complement her on her choice, I will never know.

Later, when I relived the experience in the dark and quiet of my living room after Jean and the girls went to bed, I was astonished that your fervor had been equal to mine. All I could think about was the taste of you, and the fact that I wanted more. It would always be like that for me, Sweet Heart. Even after fifteen months of intimacy; even after I had come to know every curve and crevice of your body, I could not get enough of you. And, to my utter delight and amazement, it seemed as though you could not get enough of me.

We never discussed what transpired between us at Florentina's. We didn't have to. Everything that could have been said was expressed behind the closed doors of your office or mine, where we abandoned propriety and thrilled to the feel of each other's touch. It was a happy time, of breathtaking kisses and as much foreplay as we could reasonably achieve without arousing the suspicions of our co-workers. It was gratifying, and curiously fulfilling. But, like I said, I wanted more.

September 30, 2016

I knew I was in love with you even before we went to The Mill Creek Inn. I couldn't eat, except when I was with you at Florentina's. I couldn't sleep for reliving the time spent with you and planning our next encounter. I got up early and went to bed late, most nights long after Jean retired because I felt I was being untrue to you if I shared my bed with her. I was both irritable and overly conciliatory when I was away from you, annoyed that my family obligations kept me from you and yet deliriously happy knowing that I would soon see you again. But, even though I wanted to shout my love for you from the rooftop of Cunningham, Miller, Bender and Schade, I vowed not to give voice to my feelings first. It seemed too soon in the relationship for a declaration of love and, since I knew virtually nothing about you, I secretly feared that I was simply one more dalliance for you.

Even the horror of that possibility didn't keep me from wanting you and I spent every, waking minute dreaming of our first real sexual encounter. Mentally, I blocked my every move, and your every response, until we were nothing short of Burt Lancaster and Deborah Kerr making love on a beach amidst crashing waves. That was the dream. And, then, there was the reality. Yeah. It wasn't exactly my best work since not a lot can be accomplished in the rush of excitement that evaporates in under two minutes; but, later, after we moved to the bed and found our rhythm, I think I did all right. I must have, huh? Otherwise, you never would have called me a Michelangelo, a comparison which still makes me swell with pride.

My experience with Jean had not prepared me for a woman like you. With Jean, sex had always been perfunctory and unimaginative. I think she found it distasteful, and something that had to be endured as a means to an end. With you, however, sex was joyful and uninhibited, passionate and bright; an adventure, a thing of beauty and, on every level, a spiritual experience.

We did it four times that first night. I remember that clearly because I couldn't believe I had four times in me. Even then you brought out the best in me, and the romantic. Before I met you, I would never have dreamed of luxuriating with a woman in a bubble bath or watching some sappy movie, and claiming an actor's name for my own. And I would never have blurted out an 'I love you' to a woman I had known little more than a month, when I was committed to another, for better and for worse. But with you, what once seemed unimaginable, became second-nature and right. Still, I worried about how my free-wheeling ways would affect the girls, and Jean, who, if she ever found out about us, would make my life a living hell. So, I hedged my bet and put a condition on our relationship which I was certain you would reject. That you didn't and, in fact, embraced that condition was a gift from fate who, as it turned out, would exact her price later.

In the meantime, however, I reveled in the afterglow of love and glorious sex and was struck dumb by the siren song of mind blowing orgasms. That is the only explanation for why I threw caution to the wind and agreed, no, suggested that we rent Singer's cottage the moment we found it. Having experienced paradise at The Mill Creek Inn, I was keen to find it again, and when I did, I wanted nothing less than to make it a permanent part of my life.

I loved that place, Sweet Heart. You know that I did. Not only because you were there, or because it was ours, although these were at the very top of my list of reasons, but because it was peaceful there, and beautiful, and it had a long view to the ocean which held me entranced, just as you did. I thought I would die there, possibly in the throes of a seismic orgasm, hopefully when I was old and grey, but certainly, certainly in the warmth of your arms as I transitioned to the next life. I dreamed of retiring there with you someday and, although I knew that day was far in the future and would only come after we were both unencumbered in a satisfactory way, I held that hope close to my heart even though I knew that it was probably a pipe dream. What I did not anticipate was the possibility that I would be wrenched from that place with cold-hearted indifference.

October 1, 2016

Although I was a different person when I was with you, more adventurous than cautious, more confident than not, the week we were together at the cottage I discovered a silly side of myself and I liked him. He was the guy who flexed his puny muscles while grilling bare-chested in the yard. He chased you around the house, mimicking Groucho Marx in *Animal Crackers*, and dove buck naked into the warm waters of the inlet with an enthusiastic Tarzan yell. He grew a beard and welcomed a pipe and pretended to be droll and roguish, like Noel Coward. He modeled your robe, and spoke gibberish in an awful French accent, and faked being debonair. I honestly don't know where that guy came from but, wherever it was, I hoped he never went back. You seemed to like him as much as I did, even though it was clear that you were partial to the romantic in me.

As soon as we decided to take advantage of Jean's trip to New Jersey with the girls, I made arrangements for our trip back to The Mill Creek Inn. It was tough keeping the surprise from you because we had no secrets between us and I could barely conceal my excitement at the prospect of revealing it to you. The inn was particularly meaningful for me because it was the backdrop for the metamorphosis that brought me into my own, and being there with you that first time marked a turning point in my life. For these reasons alone, it was more than a little ironic to me that our day of reckoning came so soon after we returned from that tranquil scene of our capital crime.

I arose early on the morning of our departure to carve our initials in the foremost oak in the grove of trees behind the cottage, so that I could surprise you with it upon our return. Yeah. Sappy. But I knew you would love it because it was something of permanence in a relationship that was, by its very nature, precariously impermanent.

In keeping with my plans to shower you with surprises, I wanted to present you with a ring that week, so that you would have something for your person that signified my commitment to you but I could not find what I wanted. Although I did not know exactly what that was, I knew I would recognize it when I saw it and I didn't want to settle for something that was not exactly right. When I didn't find it before our trip, I was not concerned because Christmas was on the horizon and I felt that that occasion would work just as well for what I had in mind.

When it became clear that I would have to leave you, I became obsessed with finding that ring. I spent every minute away from you searching jewelry stores and, when that didn't work, pawn shops. I got it into my mind that we were old souls who had lived and loved before, and that I had given you a ring in a previous lifetime which was out there somewhere waiting for me to find it.

By December 20th, I had scoured every conceivable source within a thirty mile radius of the city and I still hadn't found the ring. I was desperate and about to settle for something I didn't really want when I happened upon a Catholic church, Saint Rita's, holding a holiday flea market.

Expectantly, I wandered the aisles and let my eyes dart across the goods displayed on each stand before I moved on to the next. As I neared the end of the last aisle, I had given up hope, and I nearly missed it. I would have, if its owner, Sophie Palaski, hadn't called me back like a seasoned barker. Surely, she had what I was looking for she cried, as she plucked a silver ring from the tangle of jewelry that cluttered her table and held it aloft for me to see.

I knew, at once, that it was the ring. And, although Sophie spun a story about its origins, I didn't need to be told that the heart-red color of the garnets and the surrounding evergreen leaves of the band made it a symbol of everlasting love.

Sophie wanted twenty dollars for the ring, and I gave her a hundred. I would have paid ten times that amount, with a promise of more, if that was what she wanted. As a reward, she stooped and rummaged through the scramble of boxes stored under her tables and, when she stood and faced me again, she held in her hand a red, velvet, heart-shaped box. Then she took the ring from my reluctant fingers and shimmied it into the cleft designed to hold that particular piece of jewelry. I was overwhelmed by the sheer perfection of it and, although I knew that my heart would be breaking when I gave it to you, at that moment, it was happy and light.

October 5, 2016

The day I slipped that ring on your finger was the worst day of my life. I say that with certainty, knowing what came before and after. Even as the bottom fell out of my world and my stomach started churning bile when Jean told me she wanted to move, I knew that there would be worse to come and I feared I would not be equal to it.

I could barely look at Jean during the month leading up to our departure and, indeed, for most of our first year in New Jersey. It was almost as if she had sensed, somehow, that I had found happiness apart from her and had devised a way to protect her interests. But I knew better. It had nothing to do with me, and everything to do with ambition. It was a cold, calculated move, not a distraught, emotional one.

I'm an easygoing man, not given to pessimism or vengeful behavior, but in that month of days between Thanksgiving and Christmas, I discovered the dark side of my character. I would have unleashed it upon Jean unapologetically if it hadn't been for you and the girls. You were everything that

Jean was not; thoughtful and considerate, levelheaded and noble, willing to sacrifice your own happiness for that of the girls, and for Bill. That was a blow. I could not understand why, if you loved me as you said you did, you would not agree to leave Bill to be with me. It tormented me, Sweet Heart, not just then, but for many months afterwards. Had it not been for the scent of you, that arrived like clockwork every Valentine's Day, reassuring me that you were just as unwilling to let go of me as you were to let go of Bill, I would have spent the rest of my life tortured by the belief that, when it came right down to it, you preferred him to me.

I slept fitfully the night before our last Christmas Eve at the cottage. Although you convinced me that leaving you was the only rational thing to do, I was still hoping for a miracle. But, as I stood at the mouth of the inlet and stared out into the ocean, I was forced to face the fact that I'd had my miracle and would probably never see you, or that place, again. The thought sickened me and brought tears to my eyes, and I had to take a few minutes to compose myself before I could join you for our last few hours together.

Of all of the fears that plagued me that morning, the nightmare scenario was that I wouldn't be able to perform. It wasn't that I didn't want you. It was that I didn't want you just for that morning, I wanted you for a lifetime. Knowing that I was poised to spend the rest of my days without you reignited all of my old insecurities, which I thought had been extinguished when you came into my life.

The rush of emotion that overcame us when we embraced at the door was surprisingly cathartic. It cleared my mind and yours too, apparently, because you took one look at me and knew what I was worried about. To soothe me, you said, with the utmost tact and consideration, that we had plenty of time to get to *that*.

I tried to relax, thinking it couldn't get any worse, but it did. When you said that you didn't need me to come back to help you break down the cottage it wounded me, and when you said that you didn't want me to call or write, it was like you had plunged a dagger through my heart. Being able to keep in touch with you was the only sliver of hope I had left. And, although your reasoning was sound and I knew you were right, I chaffed at your assessment that there was no hope for us.

I didn't say it at the time, Sweet Heart, but I sure as hell thought it; there is *always* hope. And, for me, that hope was symbolized by the ring I had hidden in my pocket.

Your reaction when I presented it to you was everything I dreamed it would be, and I had to resist an urge to get down on one knee when I slipped it on your finger and took my solemn vow.

"I am yours and you are mine," I said. "Nothing will ever change that."

"I'll never take it off," you said. "No matter what, I'll never take it off."

And I knew that you wouldn't.

I don't know why, but it surprised me that you thought to get me something that I could always carry with me, too. That it was a medal of Raphael, the patron saint of lovers, couldn't have been more appropriate and that I could wear it next to my skin, above my heart, made me cherish it all the more.

You saw our gifts as tokens of our love, and they were. But I also saw them as symbols of hope and when you took the medal from my hands, slipped it around my neck, and made your own promise to me, I chose to invest in that perspective. When I did, the bright light of possibility swept despair from my heart and I was able to make love to you because I truly believed that it wouldn't be for the very last time.

Afterwards, we danced to "I'll Be Home for Christmas." Then I kissed you softly and walked quickly out the door. I was afraid I would start crying again and wouldn't be able to stop.

October 8, 2016

I know you think I had some grand plan to woo you with records even before I left San Francisco, but I didn't. The only plan I had was to divorce Jean and return to your arms as soon as possible, and you saw how that worked out. It wasn't that I was still in love with Jean, if I ever had been, and I would have left her in a minute if it hadn't been for the girls. They had a difficult time adjusting to their new surroundings despite their initial enthusiasm for the move. Jean was working twelve hour days and her mother imposed a level of discipline on them that even our old friend, Lance Corporal Len Cioni, would have balked at. I was the only thing that stood between the girls and the drill sergeant and I didn't have the heart to leave them to fend for themselves.

For the first few months, I was at the house when the girls got home from school. I'd listen to their stories, or help them with their homework, or take them shopping for whatever desired essential they couldn't live without. On the weekends, we looked for a house of our own. Jean was preoccupied with making a name for herself at her new office and didn't really care where we lived. I think she would have been content to stay with her parents until hell froze over, but neither the girls nor I were having any of that.

Kathleen Ann picked the house, not Jean, as you supposed. Kathleen fell in love with the Spanish architecture of the one and a half story you and Denise discovered in 1995 and selected her room while I was still looking around the living area. There were five bedrooms, so each of the girls could have their own, three bathrooms, and a grand office, which Jean would commandeer. Below grade, there was space to set up a shop and two finished rooms, one large enough for the girls to use to watch television or entertain their friends, and one half that size which I would use for a den. In the yard, there was a patio area large enough for a grill and a picnic table, and a garden. I would build a koi pond there, all the rage back then, and plant hydrangeas and daylilies and Shasta daisies, which I would often pluck the petals from to see if you still loved me or loved me not. There was a lot to recommend that house, but the most persuasive argument for it was that it was far enough away from Jean's mother to give us some breathing room.

The girls couldn't wait to show the house to Jean. They called her from a phone booth and begged her to leave the office and meet us there. She couldn't get away, she said, and couldn't understand what the hurry was. Seeing the looks of disappointment on the girls' faces, I took the phone and persuaded Jean to come and give the house her stamp of approval.

Jean left work, met us, and toured the house. She said she liked it and told the girls they did a good job in finding it. But, that night as we prepared for bed, she told me that she would not have time to set up the house or maintain it, and asked if we couldn't stay put until summer, when she expected to be more solidly situated at work.

I shook my head.

"No, Jean," I told her. "You drug us clear across the country so you could further your career, and that's fine, but the girls need roots of their own and we're going to see that they get them."

"Fine," she said. "But you're going to have to take care of everything because I can't spare the time for it."

The next day we made an offer on the house and six weeks later we moved in.

The girls were great. They banished our old furniture to the basement since it didn't conform to the style of the house, then drug me off to Macy's where we selected heavy, wood and wrought iron pieces for the living areas. Kathleen Ann took care of the kitchen, which would be her domain until she moved into a place of her own, while Sarah, Phoebe, and Grace put everything else away just as they supposed Jean would want it. When the first floor was finished, they went to work on their bedrooms and I headed to the basement to arrange the room which would become my haven, and the place where I would store and catalogue duplicates of the records I would eventually send to you. The first thing I did was set out the photograph taken of us by Lance Corporal Len Cioni, which you slipped into the pocket of my jacket while I showered on our last morning together. My happiest times were in that room, sitting in my easy chair and smoking my pipe, while dreaming of you and our cottage by the sea.

October 17, 2016

Not long after we settled in, I found a job at Morrow-Stanford, a small accounting firm just ten minutes from the house. It was a low-key office, with only four accountants and a single secretary, Inez, close to sixty. There was no rainmaking requirement and virtually no competition to rise to the top since, with only four of us on the roster, we were each as close to the top as we were going to get. I liked it there. It didn't have the energy of Cunningham, Miller, Bender, and Schade, and never would even if it quadrupled in size because you weren't there, but that suited me just fine. I'd already found the magic that was ordained for me and I wasn't looking for anything more.

I wish I could express as eloquently as you did how I felt being away from you but I am not the poet you are, so you will have to settle for this: I missed you. I was lonely and I felt incomplete, and resentful, which I tried hard to conceal from the girls but they knew something was wrong. Grace would curl up on my lap and stroke my face and tell me it was all going to be okay and

Kathleen would cook my favorite dishes, including Italian Wedding Soup, just to coax a smile from me.

The summer you were carrying Frank and preparing for his birth, I started to spend Saturdays in New York. The first time I went into the city Grace came along to keep me company and, after that, Saturdays in New York became a ritual for us. During the week Grace would plan our itinerary, scheduling a matinee or a visit to a museum, or a carriage ride in Central Park, and then Christmas season was upon us and we were shopping for presents.

Grace had a crush on her history teacher, who was a World War II buff, and she was intent on getting him a record of famous speeches given during the war. At the time, I wondered how Grace even knew that such a recording existed but, now, I know that fate must have had a hand in it because it was our search for that hard-to-find prize that led us to Ralph's Records, a little hole-in-the-wall shop off Broadway.

While Grace and the owner searched through the war era stacks, I flipped through a row of vintage 45s. I wasn't looking for anything in particular, I was just killing time; then I found "I Left My Heart in San Francisco," and time stopped.

I was staring at the title, remembering the day we met, when the proprietor came up behind me and, seeing the record in my hand, remarked that I had uncovered a treasure.

I hadn't even noticed but the disc I held had not been recorded by Tony Bennett, as I had assumed, but by Frank Sinatra! It was a rare find, I was told, since it had been withdrawn from the market only two weeks after its release to give Bennett's recording a better chance of success.

Did I know in that instant that I was going to be sending it to you for Christmas? I did. But what I didn't know then was that that simple act, born out of loneliness and longing, would lead to a lifelong obsession. Neither did I plan for you to receive the record on the first anniversary of our last day together. We have fate to thank for that, for it surely must have been the goddess Clotho herself who led me to that record at an appointed hour such that I would have just enough time to get it to you for Christmas Eve.

I didn't really expect a response from you but I was hoping against hope that I would get one. And not just a polite note of thanks, signaling that you had moved on without me, but a call perhaps, so that I could hear the tones of your sweet voice and judge for myself if I still meant as much to you as you did to me. That hope faded as each new week passed without a word from you. By Valentine's Day, I had all but resigned myself to the dreaded possibility that what we'd had in San Francisco was gone forever, and I would have to live out the rest of my life on the memory of a dream from which I had been rudely awakened.

The truth is, I didn't realize the significance of the day until your gift arrived. I was hunched over a pile of spreadsheets when Inez walked into my office.

"Looks like you got a Valentine from your old stomping grounds," she proclaimed.

I looked up, confused by what she had said until she handed the package to me and I saw your return address.

The first true smile that I had smiled since Jean broke the news that we were moving East flooded my face as I realized what it was that I held in my hand; not a letter, which had a fifty-fifty chance of being a brush-off, but a package, a thing of substance, which could only contain something wonderful and good.

I waited until Inez left the office before I tore at the wrapping and opened the box, releasing the familiar fragrance which had been encased inside. I lifted the fine, cotton handkerchief from its cradle of tissue, held it to my cheek, as you knew I would, and breathed in so deeply that it made me dizzy. I was deliriously happy, and content for the first time since I left your arms just as Sinatra finished singing "I'll Be Home for Christmas." And, in that moment, I knew that I would someday return to you and when I did, I would be backed by a choir singing that song. And that, Sweet Heart, is when I started planning my homecoming.

October 24, 2016

It began with a treasure hunt.

Although I was never a big Sinatra fan, the fact that you loved him, and that it was his record that reopened communications between us, made me decide to make Frank Sinatra my emissary. Once a year, I would dispatch him to you, charged to speak for me in a code that seemed innocent enough on its face, but was carefully chosen so you would understand its secret meaning.

I took the next day off and went back to Ralph's Records and bought every Sinatra album he had in stock; *Sinatra and Strings*, *Nice and Easy*, *Songs for Swingin' Lovers*, *Sinatra's Sinatra*, *A Jolly Christmas from Frank Sinatra*, *In the Wee Small Hours,* and *All Alone.* I gave Ralph my phone number and asked him to call me if any new Sinatra's came into his shop. Then I drove across the Hudson to Kmart where I bought myself a Soundesign freestanding audio system with an AM/FM radio, dual cassette decks, a turntable, and two speakers, all packaged nicely in a simulated, oak cabinet.

I was excited about something again and I couldn't wait to get home and assemble the system so I could listen to the music that used to make you melt in my arms.

I played *Nice and Easy* first because it contained some of our favorite songs: "Fools Rush In," "Nevertheless," "The Nearness of You" and our song, "Embraceable You." It also had the sad entreaty, "Dream*,"* and, when I listened to it, I thought to myself that if you were feeling as badly as I was, this was a song that would make you smile.

All Alone and *In the Wee Small Hours* suited my mood at the time, mournful and lonely, and throughout the 70s and 80s these albums, and others like them, such as *Where Are You*, *Point of No Return*, *Only the Lonely*, *No One Cares,* and *A Man Alone*, were my staples.

Finally, I put *A Jolly Christmas from Frank Sinatra* on the turntable and played "I'll Be Home for Christmas" for the first of a thousand times to come. I would never be able to listen to that song without tears welling up in my eyes as I imagined, again and again, every aspect of my return to you.

When we were together, you were the one who scoured stores and yard sales and flea markets for vintage Sinatra records, so I thought it ironic that this became my labor of love after we parted. It would be easier to find what I was looking for when the internet took off, and when Amazon came online in 1995 and then eBay in 1997 but, to tell you the truth, I rather enjoyed the thrill of the hunt before modern technology came into play.

At first, I didn't have a clear plan in mind. I simply started browsing the record racks in every store I could think of and, when I'd exhausted that search, I took to the phone book to find other used record shops like Ralph's. It wasn't long before I'd amassed a respectable collection and started thinking about the order in which I would send them to you. Somewhere along the line I made three important decisions; I would not send you an album I knew you already had, I would not send you the same album more than once, and I would maintain, for myself, a collection of every album I sent to you. My accountant's need for order led me to create a log of each record and every song and, when I wasn't shopping for new music, I was working on my catalogue, refining it repeatedly until I had it to a point where I could easily locate a title and its curriculum vitae.

I joined several fan clubs, and haunted libraries and book stores, both rare and modern, hoping to get my hands on a comprehensive discography. In 1977, John Ridgway published *The Sinatrafile Part 1*, and then followed up with *Part 2* in 1978 and *Part 3* in 1980. I didn't learn about them until several years later and they were published in England, which made acquiring them something of a challenge, but I persevered until I had them ensconced with my collection. These books, and others like them, were my maps to the hidden treasures I sought.

I had acquired every album Sinatra recorded by the time I returned to San Francisco. Fifty-nine were studio albums, two of which had been recorded live, and eleven were compilation albums released before he stopped recording in 1994. Some were new and still in their shrink wrap, but many were castaways, awaiting rescue. None of these contained "I Left My Heart in San Francisco." That song appeared only in *The Complete Reprise Studio Recordings*, released in a limited edition of twenty thousand in November 1995. Since I had several sources to alert me when any new releases were on the horizon, I knew when the set was in production, and pulled a few strings to ensure that I acquired one. In 2001, I discovered, on eBay, a 45 like the one I sent you in 1973 and I grabbed it because I wanted my collection to mirror yours in every way.

Of the seventy-two albums recorded by Sinatra before his swan song in 1994, eleven were off limits since we'd had them at the cottage. This left sixty-one to choose from. Of these, thirty-one made the cut; two others, *Sinatra 80 – All the Best* and *The Complete Capitol Singles Collection,* were released in 1995 and 1996, respectively. The last five I sent you were released after Sinatra died in 1998.

I faced a crossroads early on since audio cassettes had flooded the market and then again in the 80s when compact discs took off. Should I switch to the newer media or stick with the vinyl? Knowing you to be a sentimentalist, I ultimately decided to stick with the vinyl since it was more satisfyingly held and caressed than the other formats. I, however, had most of the albums in all three formats as I enjoyed listening to my favorite songs when I was driving, an activity where playback options didn't include a rack system. In 2005, I was one of the first in line to get a fifth generation iPod Classic because I recognized, as you eventually did, that iPod would give me the ability to separate the meaningful wheat from the irrelevant chaff and allow me to exist in my dream world without being distracted by music that, while good, held no significance for us.

Some of my messengers were better than others but they had one thing in common. They spoke to the pain of our separation, my constant longing, and my bright hope for the future. Naturally, I had my favorites; "Embraceable You," of course, "That Old Black Magic," "The Very Thought of You" and "Just in Time" were the songs I enjoyed most when we were together. "I'll Never Smile Again," "With Every Breath I Take," "Dream," "I Will Wait for You," I Can't Stop Loving You," and "We'll Be Together Again" were the songs that most eloquently expressed my feelings after we parted. "I Left My Heart in San Francisco" was my all-time favorite because it was the one that set me on the path back to you.

I can't begin to calculate the number of hours I spent sequestered in my den listening to the music which described my life without you. I would lift my pipe from the heart-shaped, San Francisco ashtray I picked up at the airport, on the day I left the city. I would light it with an old Zippo lighter, with Sinatra's image on it, which Ralph found when he was cleaning out his shop just before he retired. Then, I would sip Jack Daniels from the glasses you sent to mark the passing of the Chairman of the Board. That was as close to heaven as I would get until that happy day when I took you in my arms once more, and finally knew peace.

November 1, 2016

When we arrived in Union City, Sarah was seventeen, Kathleen was fourteen, Phoebe was twelve, and Grace had just turned ten. It's hard to believe that, as I write this, Sarah is nearing retirement age and Kathleen, Phoebe, and Grace are older than we were when we met. Though they are grown, and Phoebe and Grace have grandchildren, in my mind's eye they are still exactly as they were when we deplaned in Newark and went to live with Jean's parents in 1973.

Sarah was with us less than a year before she headed off to Temple to study journalism. Like you with Frank, I wanted her to attend college closer to home, but she was dead set on moving away.

In 1978, Sarah met Jim Schaeffer at a bar in Georgetown. Sarah was working for a Washington newspaper and Jim was a lobbyist with Thomas and Jay. Sarah, who inherited her mother's penchant for debate, picked a fight with Jim when she overheard him bad-mouthing FDR but it was just a ruse because Sarah thought less of FDR than

Jim did. They got married a couple of years later, in Republican splendor.

It was one of the few times that Jean slacked off her work responsibilities for one of the girls. She loved being mother of the bride and, although that probably had less to do with Sarah than it did with the fact that she got to make valuable Washington connections, Sarah benefitted nonetheless. She wanted a big, church wedding and a country club reception, which was right up Jean's alley. She and Sarah were in their elements shopping for couture gowns, tasting gourmet samples for a six course meal, and selecting just the right wine for each course. They even arranged for valet parking because, God forbid, that the guests would have to walk a few yards from the parking lot to the ballroom where the reception was held.

Sarah's wedding cost almost as much as our house, but we were making good money and could easily afford it. Jim came from old money and his parents sprang for the honeymoon in Hawaii and gifted them with a down payment for their first house in Chevy Chase. Not to be outdone, Jean paid for the furniture from her own personal account, which she had opened, shortly after we moved East, to establish her independence and further distance herself from me.

It took Sarah and Jim three years to produce their only child, James, Jr. By that time Sarah had become disillusioned with the life of a reporter and was all too happy to quit her job so that she could stay at home and plan social events for Jim's contacts and associates and, of course, raise their son. I get the impression that, these days, Sarah's marriage is more one of convenience than of undying love which, I guess, should not surprise me because, in her case, the acorn didn't fall far from the tree.

Phoebe became a high school Physical Education teacher and trains the girls' soccer team to this day. She met her husband, Vince, at the school where they both teach. They were drawn together by their mutual love of sports, although I think the fact that Vince coached the football team, and could bench-press his weight, may have had something to do with Phoebe's attraction to him.

Phoebe was much more practical than Sarah when it came to her wedding, and a lot less receptive to Jean's advice. She was not one for putting on airs but she was okay with letting us foot the bill for a pricey, though not extravagant, gown and a catered, three-course luncheon for her reception at the local Hilton. Jean still got to do her mother-of-the-bride thing when it came to the guest list and her own outfit, which some said made her look better than the bride. Since the costs for Phoebe's wedding were less than what we spent on Sarah, we paid for the Florida honeymoon and kicked in a few bucks to help with the down payment for their house.

Phoebe and Vince conceived their first child, Aimee, on their wedding night. Eighteen months later, their son, Anthony, came into the world. Aimee is married now and has two children of her own. Anthony owns a bed and breakfast in upstate New York with his partner of fifteen years, Robert.

As far as marriages go, I think Phoebe's is solid. She and Vince still work out together and spend their summers climbing mountains and running marathons; anything to stay in shape.

Grace went to nursing school and Jean was fixated on the possibility that Grace might marry a doctor. That didn't happen. Grace fell in love with Paul O'Malley, a blue-collar construction worker who eventually branched out on his own. They got married in our garden. Kathleen prepared the food for their reception and made their cake. Grace wore a vintage dress she found in a consignment shop and a halo of flowers instead of a veil. To say that Jean was disappointed that it wasn't the kind of wedding that befitted her station, as a named partner in her law firm, would be an understatement but I was thrilled not to have to dress up in another tux.

The kids went to the Poconos for their honeymoon. Before they left, I slipped them a substantial check in an amount equal to the difference between what we spent on Grace's wedding and that of her sisters. They used some of the money for the down payment on a run-down, row house in the city, which Paul re-modeled, and kept the rest in the bank until they decided that it was time for Paul to go into business for himself.

Grace and Paul have three children. Aaron, who works with his father in construction; Sam, who loves animals and became a veterinarian; and Ellie, who followed in her mother's footsteps and became a nurse.

Of everyone, I think Grace and Paul are happiest and as much in love today as they were when they married.

Kathleen Ann hated school and had no desire to go to college. She discovered her passion at an early age and doggedly pursued it, despite Jean's strong objections and unrelenting insistence that she needed to get a degree. Kathleen went to work as a line cook at a local restaurant right out of high school. She had such a natural ability with food that it didn't take her long to become a sous chef and then an executive chef at a more upscale restaurant. In 1987, when she was barely twenty-five, she opened her own place.

She started out small in an alley off the main drag in Newark but, when the building next to hers became vacant, we helped her buy it as well as the building where she had been renting space, so that she could expand. The rest is history. She has a couple of James Beard awards and a Michelin Star, but accolades don't mean much to Kathleen. For her, it's just about the food.

Of all of the girls, Kathleen had the most balance in her life, and was the most attentive. She visited us every Sunday after her lunch service and often stopped by in the middle of the week to make sure I wasn't wasting away in that big house all by myself. Kathleen never married, but when she was thirty, she adopted a little girl from China, Annie, to whom she remains devoted. The restaurant was a second home to Annie, who grew up to love cooking as much as her mother. She studied at the Cordon Bleu in France then landed a job at a little start-up in SOHO. It is Kathleen's fondest wish that Annie will someday come back to New Jersey and take over her restaurant, but she hasn't pushed her daughter in that direction. Kathleen is most unlike her mother in that regard and would never dream of trying to bend anyone to her will.

Although the girls are all different, and I can relate to some better than others, I love them equally. They were my salvation when we first moved to New Jersey, and continued to be supportive even after they married, each in their own way. We never discussed the relationship between me and their mother, but they knew the score. This colored the relationship Phoebe and Grace had with Jean in an unfortunate way, and even Sarah distanced herself from Jean as she got older, but I think this had less to do with me than it had to do with the fact that Sarah is her mother's daughter in a lot of ways.

Sometimes I can't believe that Jean and I were ever in a place where we could produce four beautiful daughters, but that was long before Jean went back to work and got ambitious. After that, everything changed.

November 5, 2016

Jean was carrying Sarah when I married her. Although she was eager to legitimize her situation, I don't think she ever forgave me for getting her pregnant and putting her in a position of having to make a decision she probably otherwise would not have made. I wasn't her ideal by any stretch of the imagination. I was poor and plodding and patently pedestrian, but I was also willing to marry her, which was a point in my favor. Respectability was always a big thing for Jean, and she must have felt that marrying me was the lesser of two evils. Yeah.

I never understood why Jean gave me a second glance the night we met at a party given by a mutual friend. I suspected it had something to do with the fact that she was on the rebound from a long-term relationship that ended with her getting dumped. This suspicion was more or less confirmed when Jean allowed me to sleep with her after we'd run into an old friend of hers, Beau Something-Or-Other. It was a revenge lay, plain and simple.

When she found out she was pregnant, Jean did the only thing a smart woman with everything to lose could do in 1955. She married. Though she may not have loved the idea of making me a permanent part of her life, I think she believed that she could mold me into the man she wanted me to be, but it didn't work out that way. It wasn't that I actively resisted Jean's efforts in that regard, but I am inherently easygoing and not at all driven, and nothing Jean did could change that about me.

Jean had Grace in 1962 and, unbeknownst to me at the time, she had the doctor tie her tubes after the delivery. She was already dissatisfied with domestic life and didn't want to reinforce her ties to it by having more children. She should have saved herself the pain and money. I think the sex that created Grace was the last we ever had. For sure, there was no more sex after Jean found out she was pregnant for the fourth and final time.

When Jean announced she wanted to go back to work, I was not surprised. I knew she was unfulfilled and profoundly unhappy. She did the best she could to be a good wife and a loving mother, but that wasn't who she was, just as the guy who wants to rise to the top and make his mark on the world is not who I was. I didn't fault her then, and don't now, for wanting something more out of life than diapers, bake sales, and car pools. What I do fault her for is treating us like we were beneath her.

Don't get me wrong, I knew I wasn't on Jean's level. She was brilliant, witty, and stunningly beautiful. That is what attracted me to her in the first place. But, unlike you, Sweet Heart, for whom these qualities are ingrained, Jean could turn hers on and off. This ability kept those of us who lived with her off-balance and guarded, but it served her well in the courtroom.

Jean went back to work for Hollister, Karl, and Schultz where she practiced before Sarah was born. For anyone else, an eight year absence from the law would have been an impediment to rehire. But the senior partners remembered Jean's dedication and her single-minded pursuit of the win, and they recognized that she had what it took to attract new clients to the firm.

Our next door neighbor, Irene, watched the girls while we worked but I took over as soon as I got home. I was a nine-to-fiver and never worked overtime, unlike Jean, for whom regular hours didn't exist. Jean thrived on the combat of litigation and never wanted to leave the battlefield; we were just collateral damage.

It didn't take long for Jean to position herself as first chair on important cases. I got the impression from things she said that she had stepped on some of her more seasoned colleagues to achieve this, and if she did, it didn't seem to bother her. Jean subscribed to a survival-of-the-fittest philosophy and made no apologies for muscling the competition out of the way so that she could join the big dogs at the top.

While the girls matured and flowered around her, Jean racked up an impressive array of wins, in part because she was a fierce competitor, and in part because she knew when a case was a loser and didn't take it on. Those she left to her less savvy colleagues. As her reputation grew, new clients came in asking for her by name but, in the early days, she shamelessly prevailed on every friend and associate we had to supply her with contacts she could cajole into clients. When she was offered the big promotion in New York, it wasn't just a matter of a bigger office and more money, it was that she had been invited to buy in as an equity partner on the condition that she relocate. This was why I had absolutely no leverage in trying to persuade her to stay where we were.

I don't believe Jean was having affairs before we moved east. She was too busy working her way up the ladder and she was laser focused on a coveted prize. It wasn't until she won the Chambers Antitrust case, made headlines and demanded, and received, named-partner status that that changed. Power was an aphrodisiac for Jean, and once coronated and enthroned she unleashed that side of herself, but only for similarly-situated royalty and worthy subjects, of which I was neither. It didn't bother me. After all, who was I to judge? Besides, after I met you I had absolutely no interest in sleeping with Jean. I was expected to play my part, however, and was occasionally called upon to escort Jean to a ritzy fundraiser or put on a happy, husbandly face for a firm party, but I was as relieved to get home and go back into my box as Jean was to have me there.

It took me a while to figure out why Jean never asked me for a divorce. She outclassed me, outgrew me, and out-earned me four to one and, after the girls left, she had every reason to believe that I wouldn't protest if she wanted to leave me. But, then, I realized that Jean didn't want to be overshadowed by a star with a light as bright as her own. If she had to be encumbered by a marriage to preserve her respectability, better it be with someone like me who made no demands on her.

Don't feel sorry for me about that, Sweet Heart, I was just as bad as she was. I used her every bit as much as she used me, but what I wanted was cover so that I had somewhere to camp out until you were ready to have me come for you. I knew you would never leave Bill and, as we grew older, I highly doubted that you would be willing to pick up where we left off and rekindle our affair. Too much had happened with you in the intervening years.

November 8, 2016

There's no easy way to break this news, so I'm just going to say it. I knew about Frank. Not from the beginning, and not for a lot of years after you had him, but when he was sixteen and almost died, I found out. How? Denise told me.

I know you're going to want to be mad at Denise, but you shouldn't be. Even though you told her not to call me, she was worried that Frank might need something from me to survive, and she knew that you would never forgive yourself if he died because you hadn't acted on that possibility. Besides, I gave her enough grief for the both of us.

I was alone in the house, getting dressed for work, when I got the call. The girls were grown and gone by that time and Jean had already left for the office. So, it was just me, moving slowly and thinking about my itinerary for the day when the phone rang. Denise explained who she was and got right to the point. She said that you had a son who had been in a car accident, and that he was in critical condition. I was slow on the uptake but, when what Denise was saying finally registered, my first reaction was shock that you had slept with Bill and produced a son. Asinine, I know, and childish, but there it was.

Denise must have known what was going through my mind because she moved quickly to set the record straight.

"No, no," she said. "It's not what you think. Frank is *your* son, Lee. It's *your* son who was in the accident."

I don't think I have ever been more dumbstruck in my life. I sat heavily on the bed and stared at the wall in front of me.

"What?" I stammered. "What? *My* son? Are you sure? There must be some mistake."

"No mistake, Lee," Denise assured me. "She found out she was pregnant after you left and... but, listen, none of that is important right now. I just wanted you to know in case you have to get out here in a hurry."

It took a few seconds to sink all the way in, but once it did, I wanted nothing more than to be in San Francisco.

"I'll be on the next plane," I said. "Just tell me where to come."

"NO!" Denise shouted into the phone. "No, for God's sake, don't come yet. She doesn't know I called you and if you show up before I tell her, it will just make matters worse. Stay where you are. I'll be heading back to the hospital in a few hours and I'll call you as soon as I know more."

Although I wanted every scrap of information there was to be had, I knew that Denise was right and there were more important things to consider than what I wanted in that moment.

"All right," I said. "I'll stay by the phone, but you have to promise to call me as soon as you know something."

Almost twelve hours went by before I heard from Denise again. I spent most of that time sitting rigidly by the phone while I tried to understand why you didn't call me the minute you found out you were pregnant. It shook me to my core to know that you kept such important news from me for sixteen years. But, by the time Denise called back, I had regained my footing and I knew what I had to do.

Denise barely finished saying that Frank was awake and doing well before I told her that I had booked a flight and would be in San Francisco the next day. She tried to dissuade me from coming, but there was nothing she could have said that would have stopped me. The best she could do was get me to agree to meet her before I went to the hospital, which I did reluctantly because, by that time, I was hell bent on talking to you and seeing our son.

Denise met me at the airport and drove me to a hotel close to the hospital where she brought me up to date and answered all of my questions. It hurt to know that you had seduced Bill and passed my son off as his, but I recognized that you were in an impossible situation and were just trying to do the best that you could for all of us. I like to think that we would have figured it out, but I could see how you'd think that more harm than good would have come of my knowing. I got that. I didn't like it, and I didn't agree with it, but I got it. What I didn't get was why you didn't tell me after we reconnected. Surely, at some point in the sixteen years we had been in communication, you could have included a note with one of your Valentine gifts.

"Oh, yeah?" Denise demanded. "And *surely* you could have written a note of your own, or called, or come running when Grace moved out and you had nothing left to keep you in New Jersey." She sniffed derisively. "If you ask me, the two of you have had your heads up your asses for a very long time."

Hearing the truth like that, inelegant and un-finessed, startled me and, sensing that she had an advantage, Denise pressed it.

"Look, Lee," she said. "I'm sure you both have your reasons for keeping things the way they are. Maybe you should think about those before you go barging back into her life like a bull moose in heat."

She had a point. Why *had* I not called or returned to San Francisco to reclaim the love of my life after Grace left? By that time, Jean was engaged in an extra-marital affair of her own and may have welcomed a divorce. So why was I content to spend all of my free time dreaming of you when I could have had the real thing? It wasn't that I couldn't leave the girls; they were self-sufficient and settled and didn't need me. And it wasn't that I couldn't leave my job. Hell, with my resume I could have easily found something comparable or better on the West Coast. What was it then that kept me in the East when I could have basked in the warmth of the Pacific with you in my arms?

I could feel the tears well up in my eyes as I faced the truth. I was afraid that you wouldn't want me, that you had moved on and liked things the way they were, a fond memory, an innocent annual flirtation, a footnote in the book of your life. How sad was that? How pathetic? Who in the hell did I think I was? And what in the hell did I think I was doing, riding to the rescue of a woman who hadn't even wanted me to come?

I took a deep breath to steady myself.

"Denise, what can I do? I can't go home without seeing them. Not now that I know I have a son, not when I'm this close to the woman who's been everything to me since the moment I met her."

Denise considered it.

"Well," she said, "If all you want to do is see them, and not confront them, or try to intrude yourself in their lives, I think I can arrange that. But I'm warning you, Lee, no funny stuff. If you hurt them, I'll make you regret it."

I believed her.

The next day they released Frank from intensive care and that night, long after visiting hours were over, Denise rushed me past the empty nurses' station and into Frank's room.

I stood by the door, away from him, for the longest time. Finally, Denise beckoned me to join her by Frank's bedside. He looked like me, younger, and certainly more handsome, but there was no mistaking that he was my son. I wanted to stroke his face or touch his arm, but I stopped short of making contact for fear that I would wake him.

"Don't be a pussy," Denise whispered. "He won't break. And if you're going to do it, you should do it now because we really have to get out of here."

Hesitantly, I took Frank's hand and stared at him intently, to burn his image into my brain. I smoothed his hair away from his forehead and kissed him softly above his brow. Satisfied that I did what I came to do, Denise disengaged my hand from Frank's and ushered me out of his room.

Seeing Frank made it worse. I didn't want to leave, particularly not when he was in such bad shape. But a deal was a deal, and I knew that he was in good and loving hands, and that there was nothing I could do for him that you wouldn't do. The next day I sat in Denise's car, across the street from the hospital, and watched as you and Bill hurried inside. More than anything, I wanted to wrest you away from Bill and claim you as my own. But, of course, I didn't. Denise and I lingered for a moment and then she started the car and drove me to the airport.

November 17, 2016

I was despondent when I boarded the plane for New Jersey after I saw Frank. It wasn't because I had longed for a son to carry on the family name or had dreamed of having a boy so I could teach him how to fish and throw a football. Those thoughts never occurred to me. Like most men about to enter the sacred order of fatherhood, my prayer was simply for a healthy baby, with a full set of fingers, and a full set of toes. Gender was not a consideration for me and I can honestly say that I was thrilled each time the doctor announced that Jean had been delivered of a daughter. I had no regrets on that score.

Nor had I ever secretly wished for a child who looked like me, and shared my passions, such as they were. The truth is that I was delighted that all of the girls resembled Jean, who had the classic good looks of a patrician noblewoman, and I was thankful that they were secure enough to pursue their own interests, which matched neither mine nor Jean's. No, it wasn't that Frank was a boy who was my spitting image that filled me with regret. It was the fact that he was created, not to fulfill a desire for parenthood but as all children should be, in the magic of a moment filled with overwhelming love, which I would never be able to experience a hundred times over as I watched him grow to manhood.

I knew, of course, that you and Bill did not have children and that you believed you were incapable of welcoming a child into your womb. Because of this, we did not have to concern ourselves with the practical matter of birth control and were free to indulge our appetites without the worry of unintended consequences. At the time, I never gave a thought to the possibility of having a child with you, because it didn't seem to be an option. Had I known that it was, I honestly don't know if I would have broached the subject with you. But now, now that I knew that that possibility had existed all along, I felt deprived of yet another chance at happiness. How cruel of God, how heartless and cold, to have let my DNA mingle with yours and create the perfect blend of our mated souls, only to keep Frank from me and allow another man to claim what was mine for his own.

Suddenly, I hated Bill with the same white-hot loathing you felt toward Jean when you learned that she would take me from you. Later, when I read your journal and discovered all of the ways in which Bill had been a father to my son, I was filled with an enormous sadness and a longing for all that I had missed. Even the fact that Bill knew that he hadn't fathered Frank, but had accepted and loved him anyway, did little to lessen my resentment. As selfish and petty as this will sound, when stacked up against Bill's incredible goodness, the truth is that I think I would have preferred it if Bill had divorced you and left you to raise Frank on your own. Had that been the case, I would have stood a reasonable chance of enjoying life as a family with you and Frank.

Yeah, I know. It would have been a longshot. And, I can almost hear you chiding me for ignoring the fact that I already had a family. But, I didn't really. Yes, I had a wife and children, but we were hardly a family. We did not establish holiday traditions, not even when the girls were young, because Jean was always absent if not physically, then mentally. We did not keep in touch with Jean's parents or look forward to annual reunions. We did not take leisurely Sunday afternoon drives through the country and stop for ice cream on the way home. We did not go on picnics or attend parades, or go on vacations except for the one we took to Yosemite, and that only happened because Jean wanted to scope out a potential, corporate client who was headquartered nearby. We didn't pick out Christmas trees, or run trains around a track, or build treehouses, or, together, teach the girls how to ride a bike. Hell, we didn't even have a dog. But you and Frank did all of those things. With Bill. Bill was the glue that bound you all together. He influenced you; protected you; nurtured you; championed you. He was all of the things I could have been and none of the small and petty things that I was.

These unworthy thoughts taunted me and filled me with shame for having thought them. Bill was an unsung hero, and the center of Frank's world; the most I would ever be where Frank was concerned was an outsider, furtively looking in. And that was only possible because of Denise.

November 24, 2016

On the way to the airport, Denise and I struck a bargain. I would not tell you that I knew about Frank, or try to contact him, and she would send me photographs and let me know what was going on in his life. Denise was true to her word, and I was to mine, substantially.

I didn't pull any funny stuff since there was, after all, Denise to be reckoned with if I did. But I was in the background when Frank gave his high school's valedictorian speech, and when he graduated from Rutgers and Rutgers Law. I visited the campus when Frank was an undergrad as often as I could, and when he was in law school, I drove by the little apartment he maintained just outside of Newark, hoping to get a glimpse of him. I stood on the outskirts of the TWA lounge when Frank was scheduled to fly home for holidays and summer vacations, and my heart ached as I watched him board that last flight that took him away from me forever and back home to you. The last time I saw Frank until we officially met for the first time, on Christmas

Day in 2011, was when he married Kris Ann. I was in the park, across the street from the church, as proud and happy as any father of the groom would be. Afterwards, I went inside and searched the pews for a forgotten program and collected a handful of the rose petals that had been strewn on the floor in Kris Ann's path. Then I drove to the reception and sat in my car until Frank and Kris Ann emerged from the banquet hall and ran to their limousine in a hail of rice. Denise would say it was pussified, and I would have to agree. But, under the circumstances, it was the best I could do.

Over the twenty-three years between the night I visited Frank in the hospital and the day I was finally able to shake his hand, I spoke with Denise often, and regularly received cards and letters from her to tell me what was going on in Frank's life, and in yours. Periodically, I received photographs; of you, always smiling, ever beautiful, and of Frank, when he won his first case and when he became a father, of Kris Ann in maternity clothes, and of my grandchildren, Michael and Mary Ann, on every one of their birthdays. It was hard to see you all so happy without me, and I envied Bill his place by your side and standing proudly behind Frank. It was a bitter pill to swallow and I doubt that I would have been able to choke it down if Denise hadn't always included a note to say that you talked about me often, and dreamed, as I did, about how it would be for us someday. I cherished those morsels of information, Sweet Heart, and looked forward to them, even though they never failed to come without Denise's take on our situation. She thought we were both crazy and that you were as much of a dumbass as I was.

December 1, 2016

It wasn't that Denise didn't love Bill. She did, especially after she learned that he knew about Frank but chose to stand by you and accept Frank as his son. But she knew that there was a hole in your heart that only I could fill and after Bill died she urged me to come for you. Believe me, Sweet Heart, I wanted nothing more, but my circumstances had taken a turn for the worse and, once again, what I wanted was overshadowed by my moral obligations.

We had been retired for a number of years and, although I welcomed the time to work on my record collection or feast upon the photographs of you and Frank, Jean couldn't sit still and filled her days with charity work and social engagements. She had always been distant and short tempered but, after a few years, she began to withdraw from me even more, and experience mood swings that became increasingly difficult to deal with. Before long, she started to accuse me of hiding her car keys and plotting against her and then, one afternoon when we were sitting on the patio talking about going to Kathleen's restaurant for supper, she forgot who her daughter was. I knew that was a bad sign, and so did Jean.

She refused to be tested for dementia and forbad me from mentioning Alzheimer's, but we both knew that something like that was going on. Though we had not had a close or loving relationship since before Grace was born, I knew she was horrified by the decline of her cognitive abilities, and I felt sorry for her. I wanted to help her in any way I could and Jean capitalized on that by making me promise never to put her in a home, no matter how bad it got. I made her that promise, Sweet Heart, because, regardless of what we were or weren't to each other, we had stayed together for more than fifty years and I owed her something for that, and for giving me four beautiful daughters who helped me get through one of the darkest periods of my own life.

It wasn't easy, especially in the last year, but we got through it with the help of a live-in caretaker. Though the girls visited her often, Sarah, Phoebe, and Grace came primarily to make sure that I was okay. Only Kathleen had been steadfast and true, no matter how neglectful and critical Jean was of her. When the end came, it was a relief for all of us, but I suspect mostly for Jean, who I am sure would have found a way to end it sooner if only she had remembered how to do it.

A few days after the funeral, Kathleen came to the house with a basketful of food from her restaurant. She was sure that I wasn't eating and knew that I couldn't say no to her cooking. Over lunch, we talked about Jean's legacy to her family, and to the law, and about the future and how I planned to spend it now that I was alone for the first time in five decades. Of course, I knew what the future held for me; I had been planning it for a lifetime. And now that my obligations to Jean, and yours to Bill were fully satisfied, it was time to put that plan in motion. But I broached the subject carefully.

"I'm thinking about moving back to California," I said. "I have some friends there, and I like the climate, and I think I'd like to spend whatever time I have left in a little cottage by the Pacific."

"*Really*?" Kathleen asked. "That's pretty far away from your family, Pop. Are you sure you don't want to stay here with us?"

"And do what?" I responded. "You girls all have lives of your own and the last thing you need is to have me underfoot. I'll be fine out there. Great, really. And, besides,

San Francisco is only a five hour plane ride away."

Kathleen studied my expression to see if it betrayed any hint of what was really going on. She knew me well enough to know that it was unlike me to pull up stakes and go off on an adventure.

I smiled at her.

"It'll be fine, Kathleen. You and your sisters will visit me often and when you can't, we'll text and Skype and it'll be just like it is now. You won't even know that I'm three thousand miles away."

Kathleen nodded. She didn't love it but, as always, she was fully supportive.

"When are you going?"

"Soon," I told her. "Before the end of the year."

And, when I said those words, I smiled broadly as I envisioned the joy that was about to come my way

December 5, 2016

Jean died on August 14th and, although I wanted to catch the first flight out of Newark, I had a timeline in mind and preparations to make.

First and foremost, I started re-growing the beard I shaved off the morning we left San Francisco. Although I loved it because you did, Jean hated it, and I was damned if I was going to give her a reason to complain about anything having to do with you.

There were also the girls to consider. I wanted them to be comfortable with my decision and spent as much time with them as they could free up in their busy lives. They needed to know that I would be all right out in the wilds of California, and I knew that I'd accomplished that mission when Grace observed that I was happier than she had seen me since we moved to New Jersey.

I let the girls go through the house and take whatever they wanted to remind them of Jean, and the good times they had there, but I didn't empty the place or put the house on the market. With Bill gone, I was optimistic that you would welcome me back into your life, but I wanted something to retreat to if you didn't. I may have matured, and built up a decent measure of self-confidence, but I still imagined the worst even as I hoped for the best.

Since there was only so much I could do from New Jersey, Denise played a big part in helping me execute my master plan. She found the carolers and held auditions for a Sinatra look-alike, and she put out an all-points bulletin for a Chevy Impala with a bench seat like the one you used to love to ride around in with me. It took Denise longer than I supposed it would to find one, and when she did, it was in bad shape. I'm not even going to tell you how much it cost to buy the car and have it restored, but I will say that when I finally laid eyes on it, I knew it was worth every penny I'd spent.

There were other details to attend to as well and tackling them with Denise did not always go smoothly. She thought the carolers should be dressed in nineteenth century period costumes and I didn't, and we disagreed on the choice for the guy who played Sinatra. She wanted the guy who looked most like him and I wanted the guy who sounded most like him. When we couldn't agree, she had to send out another casting call and, I'll give her this, she stayed with it until she discovered a college kid who fit both bills.

Denise also wanted to recruit the carolers from her church choir, but I was against it because you attended the same church and I was afraid that one of them would spill the beans. She won that one by assuring me that no one would spoil my surprise, or else they would have her to contend with and, having experienced that side of Denise first hand, I knew her assurance was as good as gold. I, however, won the costume debate. The Sinatra kid would dress like Sinatra did on the cover of his holiday album, *A Jolly Christmas*, and the backup singers would wear whatever assortment of heavy coats and hats Denise could find in the thrift shops, which was no easy task, as she was wont to remind me at least three times a week.

Though Denise was on board with having the carolers sing "I'll Be Home for Christmas" at the key moment, and she didn't gripe about finding a chime to preface the song like was used in the album, she wasn't thrilled with my choice of "The Christmas Waltz" for the lead in or "Have Yourself a Merry Little Christmas" for the send off. She thought I should use "I've Got My Love to Keep Me Warm" and "Baby It's

Cold Outside" from *The Classic Christmas Album*, but I vetoed that idea. I'd sent you "The Christmas Waltz" in 1993 and "Have Yourself a Merry Little Christmas" in 1998, the year Sinatra died. Denise's picks had no meaning for us, and a little comic relief was not in my plan.

By Thanksgiving everything was in place and all I had to do was wait. That was the hardest part of all.

The girls didn't understand why I couldn't delay my trip to California until after Christmas, but that was easily handled when I reminded them of all the years they skipped Christmas with me and Jean to be with their friends. Phoebe wanted to know if I had a hot date for Christmas Eve and when I laughed and said it was something like that she was smart enough to let it go before I told her more than she wanted to know. I celebrated Christmas with the girls and their families on the eighteenth and, the next day, I boarded the plane that would carry me back to you.

The time sped by once I was in California. I met the carolers and had them listen to Sinatra's version of the songs I wanted them to sing so that they could capture as many of the nuances of the recordings as possible. I planned to make the kid who was playing Sinatra watch You

Tube footage so he could nail Frank's expressions and mannerisms, but he beat me to it and already had the Chairman of the Board down pat. Over lunch, I told them all a PG-13 version of our story and, although it didn't exactly bring tears to their eyes, it did vest them heavily in their mission.

I claimed the Impala and headed off to see if Florentina's was still around. When I discovered it was, I arranged to pick up our favorite meal on Christmas Eve, in the hope that we would be able to share it later that evening. Then it was off to the florist where I had a hell of a time convincing the proprietor that I wanted hydrangeas, and daylilies, and Shasta daisies, not poinsettias or roses. It was good that I made that stop early in the week because it took several days for the shop to procure the flowers I wanted.

My last stop was the cottage. I was pretty sure that it had been bulldozed or sold to a developer who'd turned it into a condominium, so I was flabbergasted to find it still standing, and more than a little surprised that John Singer's son, Alan, now owned it. It took some doing but Alan finally agreed to sell it to me when I agreed to part with every cent of Jean's insurance money to get it. I gave Alan a good faith deposit and spent the day sitting in the dirt by the mouth of the inlet, hoping that you would want to live there with me and trying to decide what in the hell I was going to do with that expensive piece of property if you didn't.

We had planned for Denise to accompany me on my missions, but she fell and broke her hip a few days before I arrived in California. She was irritated to no end that she couldn't help me dot the i's and cross the t's, but I kept her posted on my progress with frequent calls and late, evening visits. I was trying to figure out how I could spring her from rehab long enough to witness the big reunion but, true to form, she had taken care of that detail herself by prevailing on one of her friends in the choir to link her in via Skype. She'd also hired a videographer to record the whole thing, an inspired bit of minutiae that paid sweet dividends when Denise presented us with a copy the next Christmas Eve.

I went back to the cottage, on the morning of the twenty-fourth, and scavenged through it for a few pieces of weathered wood. It had occurred to me the night before that I should make a FOR-SALE-INQUIRE-AT-SINGER'S sign for the front yard. It took me a while to bind the wood together, paint the sign and hammer it into the ground, and then it was time to pick up the food and the flowers. When that final bit of preparation was concluded, I went back to my room and prayed; to Jean, for forgiveness, and to Bill, for permission, and to God, for a good outcome.

I dressed early and drove out to your neighborhood where I paced in the street, at the corner of your block. I was as nervous as a sixteen year old about to pick up his first date, which was totally ludicrous for a guy over eighty who was about to reunite with a woman he had known intimately in body and soul.

When the time came, and I was assembling the carolers, it suddenly occurred to me that I was making a big mistake. I was trying to figure the odds of rejection when my cell phone rang. It was Denise.

"Go get her, Lee," she said, which, for some reason, tipped the odds in my favor and calmed me down.

I started to cry as soon as the carolers launched into "The Christmas Waltz" and we started walking toward your house. Although I knew that there was nothing less appealing than a blubbering old man, I was so overcome with emotion that I couldn't help myself. One of the carolers was primed to ring your doorbell if you didn't come outside before the first song ended, but just as she started toward your porch, there you were, smiling and clapping and about a beautiful as I had ever seen you. I think I would have pushed through the singers, and spoiled the big surprise, if the Sinatra kid hadn't sensed what was going through my mind and put his hand on my arm to stop me.

You knew what song was about to be sung as soon as the chime sounded. I could see that you were struggling to maintain your composure when the kid walked to the front of the group and started singing.

'Oh, baby, baby, you ain't seen nothin' yet,' I thought to myself, thinking of Sinatra.

I only had to wait fifty-nine seconds for my cue, but it seemed like forever. And then it was time, and I made my way through the group, loaded down with our favorite flowers and Italian Wedding Soup, which I dropped to the ground the moment I stepped onto your porch so that I could take you in my arms and experience the thrill of you once more.

December 8, 2016

Any doubts I had about your reaction evaporated the second my lips met yours and you returned my kiss with the intensity I remembered from our younger days. The carolers stopped singing and clapped and cheered with such enthusiasm that it embarrassed us. You wanted to invite them all in for hot chocolate and cookies, which was okay with me, but Denise had foreseen that possibility and had given them strict instructions to decline any such invitation. God bless Denise.

Standing as close together as we could get, with our arms around each other and smiling from ear to ear, we listened appreciatively as the carolers sang "Have Yourselves a Merry Little Christmas" and strolled back up the street to their cars.

As for what came next, do I really have to remind you? Wouldn't it suffice to say that I was able to perform, and that there is something to be said for the gentler pace of love made by a couple slowed by age? I sure hope so, Sweet Heart, because I just cannot bring myself to describe that aspect of our reunion, not even here in these private pages, intended only for your eyes.

Afterwards, we went downstairs and heated the soup and warmed the bread, which took longer than it should have because we stopped what we were doing frequently to come together for a soulful kiss or a loving caress.

We ate sitting side by side at the kitchen table, and though our bodies were touching at every conceivable point, you would periodically stop sipping soup to stroke my face or press your cheek to mine, which thrilled me immensely, and made me want to carry you back upstairs.

Although it was very late, after we ate we called Denise. I'd explained that, after Jean died, I had tracked Denise down to help with my preparations, so you were not surprised when I suggested we call her. She made you describe what happened from beginning to end and, when it was my turn to talk, she demanded to know if I had popped the question.

"Not yet, Denise," I said. "And I know, don't be a pussy."

We got very little sleep that night, but adrenaline carried us into the next day. I was nervous about proposing, and about meeting Frank, but that was a waste of good energy. You accepted my proposal without a moment's hesitation, and Frank was every bit as accepting and gracious as I hoped he would be. A week later, when we told him that we were getting married, he couldn't have been happier for us.

Fatigue finally overcame us when Frank and Kris Ann and the kids left to go home. We went to bed early and slept late into the next day, a wonderful indulgence that would become a habit in our lives. Over breakfast, you invited me to move in with you while we decided what to do next. Though I had not presumed that such an invitation would be forthcoming, I had hoped that it would.

I cleared the table and washed the dishes while you got dressed, a trivial bit of domesticity that made me feel at home. Still, I did not want to live there with you forever. It was every bit as much Bill's house as it was yours, and I wanted us to have a place that was entirely our own.

When we drove out to the cottage the next day, I shamelessly let you believe that we were revisiting it for the first time together, and that it was still for sale, even though I had purchased it a few days before. It wasn't until you decided on your own that we should buy it and live there together that I told you it was ours and always would be.

Since I wouldn't agree to let you reimburse me for half of the cost of the cottage, you suggested that we co-mingle our finances even before we married. Unlike Jean, you did not believe that we should maintain separate bank accounts, an old school philosophy that endeared you to me all the more. The timing of when we opened our joint account would not have been an issue if we had adhered to my plan to run off to City Hall as soon as possible, but you wanted to be married at the cottage, and it would take a number of months to raze it and rebuild. I worried that something would derail our wedding and leave the particulars of our lives hopelessly entangled, but we took care of that concern easily enough by having a lawyer draw up papers to give us the power of attorney for each other, and new wills that took care of our kids in an equitable way. It wasn't that we thought that Frank, or the girls, wouldn't want to do the right thing if we died before we were married, but we didn't want there to be any question as to what our intentions were.

It turned out to be a good thing that we decided to wait to tie the knot. Although Frank was delighted that you found love again and would not be alone, the girls needed time to get comfortable with the idea that I wanted to remarry. They did not have an obsessive allegiance to their mother, but she was their mother nevertheless, and she had been gone just five months when we broke the news to them.

I returned to New Jersey with you by my side just after the start of the new year. We decided that you would accompany me so that you could meet the girls in person and help me get my house ready to market. I was relieved that we were in unison on this because there was no force on earth which could have compelled me to leave you behind again if you hadn't wanted to make the trip. In that event, I would have Skyped the girls and hired a property manager to handle the sale of the house. It wouldn't've been ideal, but I wasn't taking any chances.

The girls were reserved when they met you, at Kathleen's restaurant. We felt it would push their limits to learn about you, for the first time, in the house that had belonged to their mother and we didn't want that factor to exacerbate what we knew was going to be an already stressful situation.

We told them that we worked together at Cunningham, Miller, Bender, and Schade, and kept in touch after I moved east. We did not divulge the true nature of our relationship, but rather led them to believe that our long-distance friendship blossomed into love after Jean died and I returned to California.

They peppered us with questions and urged us to take more time to get to know each other again before leaping into marriage. It was only when they learned that we wouldn't be making it official for several months that they let down their defenses and warily let you in.

We stayed in Union City just short of a month. You were as uncomfortable in my house as I was in yours, but you made the most of the situation by satisfying your curiosity about the life I had led without you. You were fascinated with my sanctuary and delighted to discover that I still smoked the pipe we'd purchased on our anniversary trip to The Mill Creek Inn. We spent most of our down time there, or in the adjacent room watching television, as the girls had when they were growing up. You were not surprised to find that Phoebe, Grace, and Kathleen's rooms were just as they'd left them but were confused by the spartan décor of Sarah's old room, which you expected to find the most lavishly girlish of all. It had been, I explained, until the last of the girls moved out and I took Sarah's bedroom for my own.

"Didn't Jean object?" you asked.

"No," I said, simply, and we left it at that.

We slept in that room, and never opened the door to Jean's, which the girls dismantled along with their old rooms and the living areas. You and I packed up my den, my clothes and the photographs the girls hadn't taken for themselves, and had the entire kit and caboodle shipped to California.

Though I hadn't used my Soundesign stereo in years, I was partial to it and wanted to keep it. You felt the same way about the old GE we'd rescued from Fred's Secondhand Furniture Shoppe. Since we both owned iPods, it was unlikely that we'd use either of those systems ever again, but they were so meaningful to us that we couldn't bear to release them. Grace helped us resolve that predicament by offering to keep the Soundesign in the family, and you and I kept the GE because we had purchased it together.

All of the closets and drawers and cupboards had been cleared out by the end of the first week and nothing remained but the furniture. The girls didn't want any of it and thought I should sell it, but since it was in pristine condition and complemented the style of the house, we decided to leave it in place in the hope that it would facilitate a quick sale. It did. The listing went live two days before the first open house, which was well attended and resulted in multiple offers. We accepted the one that included the furniture as part of the deal and closed escrow ten days later.

In the interim, we drove to Hoboken to stare at the spot where Sinatra was born and take the walking tour. We bought several loaves of bread at Dom's Bakery, which were every bit as good as Florentina's and shared a cheesesteak at Piccolo's. We visited the storefront that used to be Ralph's and took a ferry to Ellis Island to stare up at the Statue of Liberty. We rode an elevator to the top of the Empire State Building, took in a matinee of *Jersey Boys*, and enjoyed a carriage ride around Central Park. We spent a day and night in Atlantic City and strolled along the windy Boardwalk hand in hand. On the way back, we spent two days in Philadelphia so we could see the Liberty Bell, Independence Hall, the Betsy Ross House, and the Franklin Museum. It was as if we were on our honeymoon and we made the most of it, knowing that once we returned to San Francisco, we would never leave it again.

When we finally boarded the plane to return home, we were exhausted, but giddy with excitement to get to work on the cottage. Sarah and James, Phoebe and Vince, Grace and Paul, and Kathleen were all there to see us off. They may not have been entirely won over by your warmth and charm, but they appreciated that you had deferred to them in all things related to the house. And they could see that you loved me and that I was devoted to you. It wasn't the whole ballgame, but it was a good inning.

We didn't list your house until June because we needed a place to live while the new cottage was being constructed. While that work was in progress, we downsized everything we could in your home. I was stunned to discover that you still had our cement Lab, Max, and the blue striped blouse I had given you decades earlier, and my blue Chambray work shirt which hung in your closet so that it was easily accessible when you wanted to wear it. Frank turned out to be a sentimentalist like his mother, and happily carted box after box of treasure from your home to his. When your house finally sold, a month before we married, Frank and Kris Ann and Denise all pitched in to ready what remained for pick up by the Purple Hearts, and you and I moved into a suite at the Holiday Inn, a block from Florentina's.

But it wasn't all work and no play. We spent a heady week drawing up rough sketches of the house we wanted to share. When we were finally satisfied we took them to a builder who tweaked them just enough so that our more fanciful must-haves could be incorporated without breaking the bank. We demolished our old Blue Heaven on March 1st, which gave our builder plenty of time to complete the new cottage by September 25th, the date on which you thought we should be married. It was the date I started at Cunningham, Miller, Bender, and Schade and met you, and you loved the synchronicity of that.

We visited the construction site every day and often picnicked by the water as we watched the workers bring the new cottage to life. When the outside of the house was completed, and the feel we were going for was finally evident, we brought in a designer to come up with a plan to landscape the area with as much greenery and color as the lot could sustain. We wanted it all done well before the wedding, and had our builder and landscaper bring in extra crews to ensure that it would be.

When we weren't at the cottage, we shopped for furniture. We went to Ethan Allen for everything except the bed, and to Home Goods for nearly all of our art and accouterments. I loved it that you wanted a bed that resembled as closely as possible the one we first shared, and that you wanted it to be a double. After so many years apart, the last thing we wanted in that area of the house was more space.

Designing, building, and furnishing the cottage was the most fun we'd had in years. It made us feel young again, and like we had our whole lives in front of us.

By the time September 25th rolled around, all was in readiness. The girls, and their families, flew in from New Jersey, and thanks to regular calls and Skype sessions from you to include them in the process, they were fully on board with the wedding. They were able to come a few days early which gave them plenty of time to bond with Frank and Kris Ann and their new aunt, Denise.

They stayed in town, at the Holiday Inn, just a couple of floors down from the suite you and I were occupying. Although the new cottage was completed and filled with all of our belongings, we didn't want to move in until we were officially man and wife. I was not as keen on this idea as you were, but I recognized the value in saving something for the wedding night.

In all the time that we were together, there were only two things that we disagreed on. I wanted to buy you the biggest and most perfect diamond ring we could find, with a wedding band to match, but you wouldn't hear of it. The only ring you wanted was the one I gave you forty years earlier. So, we had it resized, at the last possible moment to minimize the time it would not be on your person, and you wore it on a chain around your neck until I placed it on the finger where it had always belonged. That issue was happily resolved, but the other one had a clear winner and loser.

Over my strong objections, you stayed with Denise the night of the twenty-fourth because you believed it would be bad luck if I saw you on the day of the wedding before the ceremony. Nothing I said could dissuade you and I finally had to relent and let you have your way. But I pushed the envelope as far as I could by refusing to drop you off at Denise's until one minute before midnight. Eleven hours later, as Sinatra sang "From This Moment On," the girls led their families from the house to the inlet, Denise served proudly as your matron of honor, and Frank escorted you up the limestone path to the water's edge and gave you to me.

If December 24, 1972 was the worst day of my life, September 25, 2012 was the best. The ceremony was beautiful and poignant and mercifully short. We took traditional vows in front of the family and saved the mushy stuff for when we were alone. Florentina's and The Tokyo Palace dropped off heaping platters of the foods we selected and everyone helped themselves and ate informally at the tables we'd had set up in front of the cottage. Early in the afternoon, the kids changed into shorts and bathing suits so they could play volleyball in the yard or swim in the water where we made love forty years earlier. Around six, I asked Frank, James, Paul, and Vince to fire up the grill and cook us each a porterhouse steak, just like the ones we enjoyed at Beefeater's. We wanted to incorporate as much of our past into the occasion as possible, and we couldn't forget Lance Corporal Len Cioni, who snapped one of the only two photographs taken of us together when we were young.

After supper, the party started to wind down and, by sunset, you and I were finally alone. Although Denise thought we should honeymoon on a cruise ship, neither of us was interested in leaving the place it had taken us so long to get back to, so we spent the honeymoon in our new home and settled into our lives as husband and wife.

December 17, 2016

The next four years were heaven on earth. We shopped the farmers' markets on the coast road and grilled in the yard in sight of the inlet. We worked in the garden and floated in the bay. We walked into St. Thomas and around the Village and then home again, just so we could hold hands in public. We burned scores of candles and took lots of bubble baths. We danced daily to the music that formed the soundtrack of our lives, and we made love with a regularity that belied our age. We never ran out of things to talk about but were equally content to sit quietly on the porch and look out into the inlet for hours on end.

During that time, I got to know Frank. He may have looked like me, but he had your sweet disposition and vibrant personality. He made friends easily, even with his adversaries in the courtroom, where you thought his style tended to be more like that of those guys on *Suits* than the ones on *Law and Order*. Although he could be thoughtful and serious-minded, which I think he got from me, he was also fun-loving and self-aware, which he no doubt got from you. He was not afraid to take big risks, but carefully evaluated his odds of success before he did, a character trait he must have picked up from Bill. Nor was he afraid to ask for advice and I was flattered beyond measure when he sought out my counsel on his run for District Attorney. He treated me warmly and would often light a cigar and join me on our glider where I smoked my pipe, while you and Kris Ann and Denise tended to the cleanup after family meals. I took advantage of every opportunity to interact with Frank but I was careful not to overstep the unexpressed boundaries that I knew existed.

Frank never asked me to go fishing with him at Lake Shasta, nor would he allow me to help him dismantle the treehouse he had built with Bill so it could be reassembled in his yard before your house was listed for sale. I did not intrude when he and you, alone, undertook to box up the last remaining items that had belonged to Bill. Nor did I take offense, or harbor a secret longing, when he chose to address me as Lee, even though Kris Ann began to call me 'Dad' the moment she found out we were engaged.

Over the years, even before we reunited, I developed a deep admiration for

Bill, and was able to let go of the resentment I felt toward him for having replaced me in Frank's life. Although I clearly knew how the all-consuming love of a woman could drive a man to do things he otherwise would not do, I highly doubt that I would have been able to do what Bill did when he chose to look the other way and took on a responsibility that was not his to bear. Understanding, at last, why you could not bring yourself to abandon Bill all those years ago, I did not wish for things that were his and not mine.

The only fly in the ointment was Denise's passing. We'd grown accustomed to including Denise in our daily lives and were happy to do it because we owed her a debt of gratitude that could never be repaid. Beyond that, Denise was an uplifting and colorful presence, a welcomed disrupter of the peace and quiet of our surroundings, and the life of any party she chose to attend. She often showed up unexpectedly to challenge our status quo by proposing a balloon ride, or a trip to the zoo, or a wine-tasting tour of the local vineyards. She described, in great comic detail, her efforts to locate a blue Chevy Impala that still had an engine in it, and your reaction when you received a record from me the year that she had taken matters into her own hands and sent me the handkerchief you could not bring yourself to send. On each Christmas Eve, she reassembled the choir to serenade us as they had in 2011, even going so far as to track down the kid who played Sinatra, who was no longer a college student, but a stock broker in San Diego.

Denise always said that she'd die of a stroke in the middle of a tirade, but she died peacefully in her sleep, in the bed she'd shared with John for more years than you and I had known each other. We took her death hard; you because you lost your best friend and confidant, and I because, without her, I may have never known about Frank or found the courage to make my way back to you.

It was an idyllic life, a long time coming, and I thanked God for it every night and prayed that it would never end. But, of course, it did.

December 24, 2016

You died in my arms on our fourth wedding anniversary. We knew it was coming. Earlier in the year, you started to retain water and began to tire easily. You developed a hacking cough and, at times, your breathing was labored and shallow. When you began to experience episodes of dizziness and nausea, you finally agreed to see a doctor, but by then the damage had been done. You were diagnosed with end stage, congestive heart failure and our days together were numbered, just as they always had been.

Medication eased your symptoms, but in the months leading up to your death we rarely ventured far from the cottage. You were happiest there, and content to pass your days listening to Sinatra as you puttered around the cottage until fatigue overcame you. Then you would nestle next to me on the sofa and nap the afternoon away in the shelter of my embrace.

Despite my enormous grief, I tried to keep things light and upbeat. I brought you wildflowers from our garden and won ton soup from The Tokyo Palace, and I entertained you with bawdy tales about how our lives would have been if only we had stayed together in 1972. But, in the dead of night, while you breathed heavily beside me, I allowed the devastation I felt to wash over me like a swell, to cleanse my anguish for the coming day.

I knew the end was near when you asked me to run into town to pick up our favorite meal from Florentina's, Italian Wedding soup, fresh-baked bread, and an antipasta of exotic meats and cheeses with briny olives and sweet ripe figs that you always said came straight from the Garden of Eden. I think you knew it would be our last meal together because it was just like you to want it to be the same as our first.

You managed a few sips of soup and a bite of bread and then you said you wanted to rest. I climbed into bed beside you and gathered you into my arms and held you close to my chest, praying that the strength of my heart would flow into yours and keep you with me for another day. Sinatra sang in the background from a playlist of slow songs and, when "Embraceable You" queued up, I sang along softly, and continued singing even after you smiled and sighed and took your last breath. Your last words all but destroyed me.

"I am yours and you are mine," you whispered. "And nothing will ever change that. Take care of our son."

Although my voice cracked and waned and I stumbled over the words, I sang to you until the playlist ended, and then I called Frank. We never told him how sick you were because you didn't want to worry him. But, he could see for himself that your health was declining and he called daily to talk with you and get a status report from me. When I called him on the afternoon of the twenty-fifth he was fully prepared, but he still took it hard. It broke my heart all over again that I could not comfort him as a father would a son, but we agreed that we would never tell Frank the truth about his paternity, and I honored that decision, Sweet Heart, even though he was the only source of true solace in what had become my sad and empty life.

There was no pomp and circumstance to mark your passing, just a quiet gathering of family when your ashes came home. They will be mingled with mine and buried under our oak tree when my time comes. We decided that the ring I gave you when we parted would not be cremated with you, but would be bequeathed to Frank's daughter, Mary Ann, upon my death. The ring is to pass on to her daughter and her daughter's daughter, never to be destroyed or buried with its caretaker. Rather, it is to remain in circulation in the universe, as it had been before I found it, to ensure that it will be here waiting for us when we reincarnate, as you were sure we would.

I did not believe in reincarnation, or in fate, as the guiding force in our lives until I read the journal you wrote for me after Jean died. When I did, I could see that, from the moment our parents named us, we were meant to be together. That I was called Lee was of no consequence. In whatever realm these things are determined, we were Deirdre and Hartley, DEIR HART. And, although I was always Hartley Albert Rutherford Tate, apparently destined from birth to walk a circuitous path, it wasn't until you married Bill Reid and became Deirdre Elaine Anderson Reid that our initials formed the near-perfect acronym, DEAR HART, and the stage was set for us to strut and fret upon it. It was eerie, really, how it all came together. And now that I've had a chance to think about it, I have to admit that there is something preternaturally fitting that a disease of the heart was the thing that took you from me, a mere 1,738 days after we reunited.

Fate only gave us six years together; fifteen months when we first met and a scant fifty-seven months after I re-appeared at your door backed by a choir singing the song that marked the occasion of our deepest heartbreak and our joyful reunion. Don't get me wrong, I'm not complaining. As you often said, we were lucky to get a second chance. But, sometimes, when I sit on our porch and look out into the inlet, I wonder why we could not have met when we were young and unattached, and dream about the man I could have been if fate had not separated us for a lifetime.

Before I met you, I was an unremarkable guy, about as ordinary as they come but, with you, I was my best self, and a little like the Clark Gable you always thought me to be. That part of me was dealt a crippling blow when we parted, but I found a purpose and recovered. Now, I fear, it is gone forever or, at least until the next time that I stumble into your life and get to begin mine.

As for now, I am comforted by the belief that somewhere in that ethereal place where we were created from the same wisp of angel's breath, you are waiting for me to return to your arms. I suspect you won't have long to wait, Sweet Heart, for it is Christmas Eve, and if the course set by fate runs true to form, this year it won't be

Sinatra who comes to cheer you, it will be me.

September 25, 2017

We found Lee on Christmas day. He was on the glider on his front porch, looking out into the inlet he and my mother loved so much. The coroner said he suffered a massive heart attack the day before and, even though there was no one with him, he didn't die alone. Sinatra was there, as he always had been, singing "I'll Be Home for Christmas" repeatedly from Lee's iPod, as Lee went to join my mother for the very last time.

Lee's girls divided his life insurance and his savings, but the cottage and its contents came to me. I wasn't sure I wanted to keep it. Kris Ann and I led busy lives and, although there was something to be said for having a second home where we could go to relax and unwind, we were not big fans of nature, and the prospect of solitude and spotty Wi-Fi didn't particularly appeal to us.

A few weeks after Lee's death, we drove out to the cottage to take inventory and make a final decision about its disposition. Kris Ann was stripping the bed when she found my mother's memoir, and

Lee's, under their pillows. It was a mixed blessing.

I was surprised that my mother would write a memoir and shocked to discover a side of her I had never known. And, I was angry, furious really, that she had betrayed my father for the lion's share of their lives together and made me an unwitting co-conspirator to her lie.

It was Kris Ann who helped me put it all into perspective by pointing out that, even though Mom was in a desperate situation, she loved me from the moment she learned that I was growing inside her and gave up true love to stay with my father because she couldn't bear to hurt him. I was the luckiest man who ever lived, Kris Ann said, to have been so loved by three people that they each carried a searing pain for their entire lives so I could be happy. As for Lee, who I wanted to cast as a villain, he gave up the most, Kris Ann said, by keeping the secret of my paternity even though he was forced to watch my life unfold from the shadows; and later, after he met me, passed up the chance to assert his claim out of respect for the man who raised me. Hardly the actions of a bad guy, Kris Ann observed, and when I finally regained my equilibrium, I had to admit that she was right.

Over the next few months, I re-read the memoirs several times, always at the cottage, sometimes alone on the porch, but often with Kris Ann curled up beside me on the loveseat. My stoic, practical wife, who had always preferred Tom Clancy to Nicholas Sparks, was charmed by my mother's story and came to love the cottage, and the inlet, and the giant oak tree on which Lee had carved his initials, and Mom's, inside a sturdy heart beneath which we had buried my mother's ashes, and Lee's, in accordance with their wishes.

I was not as easily charmed. I was torn between the deep and abiding love I had for my father and my affection for Lee, who brought my mother back to life when nothing else could. Although I didn't realize it at the time, looking back on it now, it is plain to see that Lee was the love of my mother's life. It was apparent in the gestures she shared with him that I never saw her share with my father. She held Lee's hand at every opportunity and, whenever he was at the sink, she would come up behind him and nuzzle her face against his back until he turned and kissed her, properly and with a hint of passion. She caressed his arm affectionately and stroked the neatly trimmed beard on his weathered face and, whenever they drove, she sat tightly up against him on the refurbished bench seat of their cherished Impala, which now belongs to me. She kissed him openly and often, and when she looked at him from across a room, it was with an expression brimming with love. As for Lee, there was no doubt in my mind that Mom was the love of *his* life. He never took his eyes off of her, not even for an instant.

It took time but, ultimately, I realized that I had no right to begrudge my mother and Lee the tidbits of time they had together. My parents enjoyed forty-nine good years with each other, which they probably could not have done if the bond they shared was not as deep and as meaningful as the one Mom had with Lee. The nature of the relationships may have been based on different kinds of love but I came to understand that love is love, no matter what form it takes.

And, so, we kept the cottage. Kris Ann decided that we would retire there and, for as long as the trust we created to keep the cottage in the family endures, our children, and their children, and their children's children can come here too, when fate deals them a seemingly insurmountable blow, and they need to remember the magic of love.

Francis Albert Reid – Frank

The Music of Deirdre and Lee

1971   *Songs by Sinatra, Volume* 1
        "Embraceable You"
        "That Old Black Magic"

        Sinatra and Strings
        "Misty"
        "Come Rain or Come Shine"
        "That's All"

        S*inatra-Basie: An Historic Musical*
        First
            "I Only Have Eyes for You"

        Great Songs from Great Britain
        "The Very Thought of You"

        Sinatra's Sinatra
        "Call Me Irresponsible"

        Nice and Easy
        "Nevertheless"
        "The Nearness of You"
         "Fools Rush In"

        Ring A Ding
        "Let's Fall in Love"

        Come Dance with Me
        "Something's Gotta Give"

"Just in Time"

Columbia Single: "I'm in the Mood for Love"

RCA Single: "Our Love Affair"

The Concert Sinatra
"My Heart Stood Still"

1972   *Songs for Swingin' Lovers*
"I've Got You Under My Skin"
"You're Getting to Be a Habit with Me"
"Too Marvelous for Words"
"How About You"

A Jolly Christmas From Frank Sinatra
"I'll Be Home for Christmas"

1973   Reprise Single: "I Left My Heart in San Francisco"

1974   *All Alone*
"What'll I Do"
"All Alone"
"Oh, How I Miss You Tonight"
"Together"
"When I Lost You"

1975 *In the Wee Small Hours*
  "In the Wee Small Hours"
  "Deep in a Dream"
  "I Get Along Without You Very
Well"
  "I See Your Face Before Me"
  "I'll Never Be the Same"
  "This Love of Mine"

1976 *Where Are You*
  "I Think of You"
  "Autumn Leaves"
  "Maybe You'll Be There"
  "Rain"
  "There's No You"
  "Where Are You"

1977 *Softly as I Leave You*
  "Softly as I Leave You"
  "Dear Heart"

1978 *No One Cares*
  "I'll Never Smile Again"
  "A Cottage for Sale"
  "None but the Lonely Heart"
  "Stormy Weather"
  "Where Do You Go"

1979 *Point of No Return*
  "These Foolish Things"
  "Day In Day Out"

"I'll See You Again"
"I'm Walking Behind You"
"It's a Blue World"
"Memories of You"

1980   *Only the Lonely*
"Ebb Tide"
"Guess I'll Hang My Tears Out to Dry"
"One for My Baby"
"Only the Lonely"
"Sleep Warm"
"Willow Weep for Me"

1981   *A Man Alone*
"A Man Alone"

1982   *Dedicated to You*
"Always"

1983   *Sinatra at the Sands*
"The Shadow of Your Smile"

1984   *Close to You*
"With Every Breath I Take"
"Close to You"
"The End of a Love Affair"
"If It's the Last Thing I Do"
"It's Easy to Remember"

1985   *Sinatra and Company*

"My Sweet Lady"

1986   *Sinatra and Swingin' Brass*
       "They Can't Take That Away from
Me"

1987   *Reflections*
       "All the Things You Are"

1988   *Sinatra's Swingin' Session*
       "My Blue Heaven"

1989   *The Broadway Kick*
       "There but for You Go I"

1990   *My Way*
       "All My Tomorrows"

1991   *Put Your Dreams Away*
       "Dream"
       "If I Forget You"

1992   *That's Life*
       "I Will Wait for You"

1993   *Sinatra Family Wish You a Merry Christmas*
       "The Christmas Waltz"

1994   *This Is Sinatra*
       "Learnin' the Blues"

1995   *Look to Your Heart*
       "You, My Love"

1996   *This Is Sinatra, Volume 2*
       "Time After Time"

1997   *It Might as Well Be Swing*
       "I Can't Stop Loving You"

1998   *Sinatra – A Man and His Music*
       "Fly Me to the Moon"

       Christmas Songs by Sinatra
       "Have Yourself a Merry Little Christmas"

1999   *Swing Along with Me*
       "Love Walked In"

2000   *A Swingin' Affair*
       "Night and Day"

2001   *Some Nice Things I've Missed*
       "You Turned My World Around"
       "What Are You Doing the Rest of Your Life"
       "You Are the Sunshine of My Life"

2002   *Trilogy*
       "My Shining Hour"

"It Had to Be You"

2003 *The Columbia Years, Volume 6*
"If I Had You"

2004 *Sinatra 80 – All the Best*
"The Impatient Years"
"Melody of Love"

2005 *Complete Capitol Singles Collection*
"My One and Only Love"
"Fairy Tale"
"Don't Change Your Mind about Me"
"If I Had Three Wishes"
"When I Stop Loving You"

2006 *Romance*
"More"

2007 *Greatest Love Songs*
"I Hadn't Anyone till You"

2008 *I'm in the Mood for Love*
"You'll Never Know"

2009 *Songs from the Heart*
"Our Love Is Here to Stay"

2010 *Absolutely Essential Collection*
"We'll Be Together Again"

2011 *A Jolly Christmas from Frank Sinatra*
  "I'll Be Home for Christmas"

About Linda Lingle

Linda Lingle began writing at a young age and had some early success with her whimsical short stories. Then life intervened and she took a break from writing to build a career in public service. When the storyline for *Dear Heart*, and its companion book, *Sweet Heart*, came to her out of the blue, it sparked her imagination and reignited her enthusiasm for writing. She is currently working on a screenplay for *Dear Heart* which incorporates the plots of both books. Linda lives in Pennsylvania with her husband, Arthur, and her dog, Sam.

Social Media

Website: www.lindalinglebooks.com

Facebook:
www.facebook.com/LindaLingleBooks

Twitter: https://twitter.com/lindalinglebks

Google +:
https://plus.google.com/s/lindalinglebooks

Acknowledgements

Heartfelt thanks to Denise Lowey, John Singer, Patricia Miller and Jill Bender Schade, who were there at the beginning, and cheered me on until I crossed the finish line.

Thanks, too, to all of the family, friends and new-found fans who purchased *Dear Heart* and gave it a life outside of my study.

If you enjoyed this story, check out these other Solstice Publishing books by Linda Lingle:

Dear Heart

Deirdre Reid and Hartley (Lee) Tate feel an immediate attraction when they meet at the office where they will work together and fall in love. There is only one problem: they are married to others and Lee has four daughters to whom he is devoted.

For 15 months Deirdre and Lee carry on a passionate affair. Then Lee's wife is offered a big promotion across the country. With his heart breaking, Lee leaves Deirdre in San Francisco and moves East with his family so his wife can advance her high-powered career.

Soon, unforeseen circumstances have Deirdre second-guessing her insistence on a clean break. She resists every impulse to fly to Lee's side, but on the first anniversary of their parting, Deirdre grows increasingly regretful and melancholy. Then she receives a surprising Christmas present which sets in motion a 38-year ritual that, against all odds, keeps alive the love she shared with Lee.

https://bookgoodies.com/a/B07CX91BYM

https://www.barnesandnoble.com/w/dear-heart-linda-lingle/1129128146?ean=9781625267887

Made in the USA
Middletown, DE
05 August 2018